THIS WHERE'S WALLY? BOOK BELONGS TO:

HEY, WALLY FANS! FIVE INTREPID TRAVELLERS ARE LOST IN EVERY SCENE! CAN YOU FIND THEM?

ODLAW   WIZARD   WENDA   WOOF   WALLY
               WHITEBEARD

AND IN EVERY SCENE, THE TRAVELLERS HAVE EACH LOST SOMETHING PRECIOUS! CAN YOU FIND THEM TOO?

WALLY'S KEY   WOOF'S BONE   WENDA'S CAMERA

WIZARD WHITEBEARD'S SCROLL   ODLAW'S BINOCULARS

For Wally

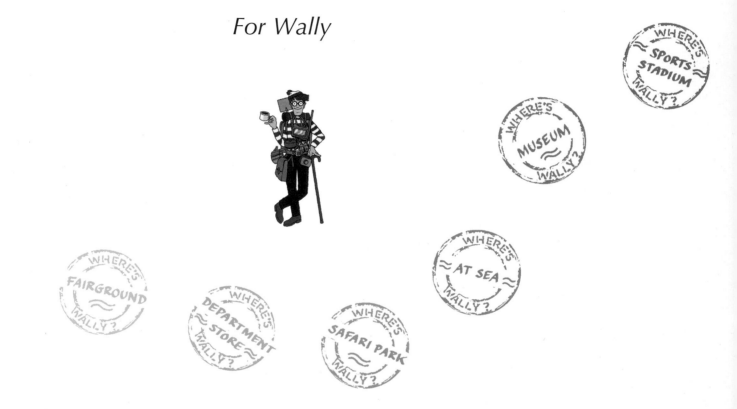

First published 1987 by Walker Books Ltd
87 Vauxhall Walk, London SE11 5HJ

This edition published 2016

28 30 29

© 1987 – 2016 Martin Handford

The right of Martin Handford to be identified as author/illustrator
of this work has been asserted by him in accordance with the
Copyright, Designs and Patents Act 1988.

This book has been typeset in Wallyfont and Optima.

Printed in China

British Library Cataloguing in Publication Data:
a catalogue record for this book
is available from the British Library.

ISBN 978-1-4063-0589-0

www.walker.co.uk

MARTIN HANDFORD

WALKER BOOKS

AND SUBSIDIARIES

LONDON • BOSTON • SYDNEY • AUCKLAND

HI FRIENDS!

MY NAME IS WALLY. I'M JUST SETTING OFF ON A WORLDWIDE HIKE. YOU CAN COME TOO. ALL YOU HAVE TO DO IS FIND ME.

I'VE GOT ALL I NEED – WALKING STICK, KETTLE, MALLET, CUP, RUCKSACK, SLEEPING BAG, BINOCULARS, CAMERA, SNORKEL, BELT, BAG AND SHOVEL.

I'M NOT TRAVELLING ON MY OWN. WHEREVER I GO, THERE ARE LOTS OF OTHER CHARACTERS FOR YOU TO SPOT. FIRST FIND WOOF (BUT ALL YOU CAN SEE IS HIS TAIL), WENDA, WIZARD WHITEBEARD AND ODLAW. THEN FIND 25 WALLY-WATCHERS SOMEWHERE, EACH OF WHOM APPEARS ONLY ONCE ON MY TRAVELS. CAN YOU FIND ONE OTHER CHARACTER WHO APPEARS IN EVERY SCENE? ALSO IN EVERY SCENE, CAN YOU SPOT MY KEY, WOOF'S BONE, WENDA'S CAMERA, WIZARD WHITEBEARD'S SCROLL, AND ODLAW'S BINOCULARS?

WOW! WHAT A SEARCH!

Wally

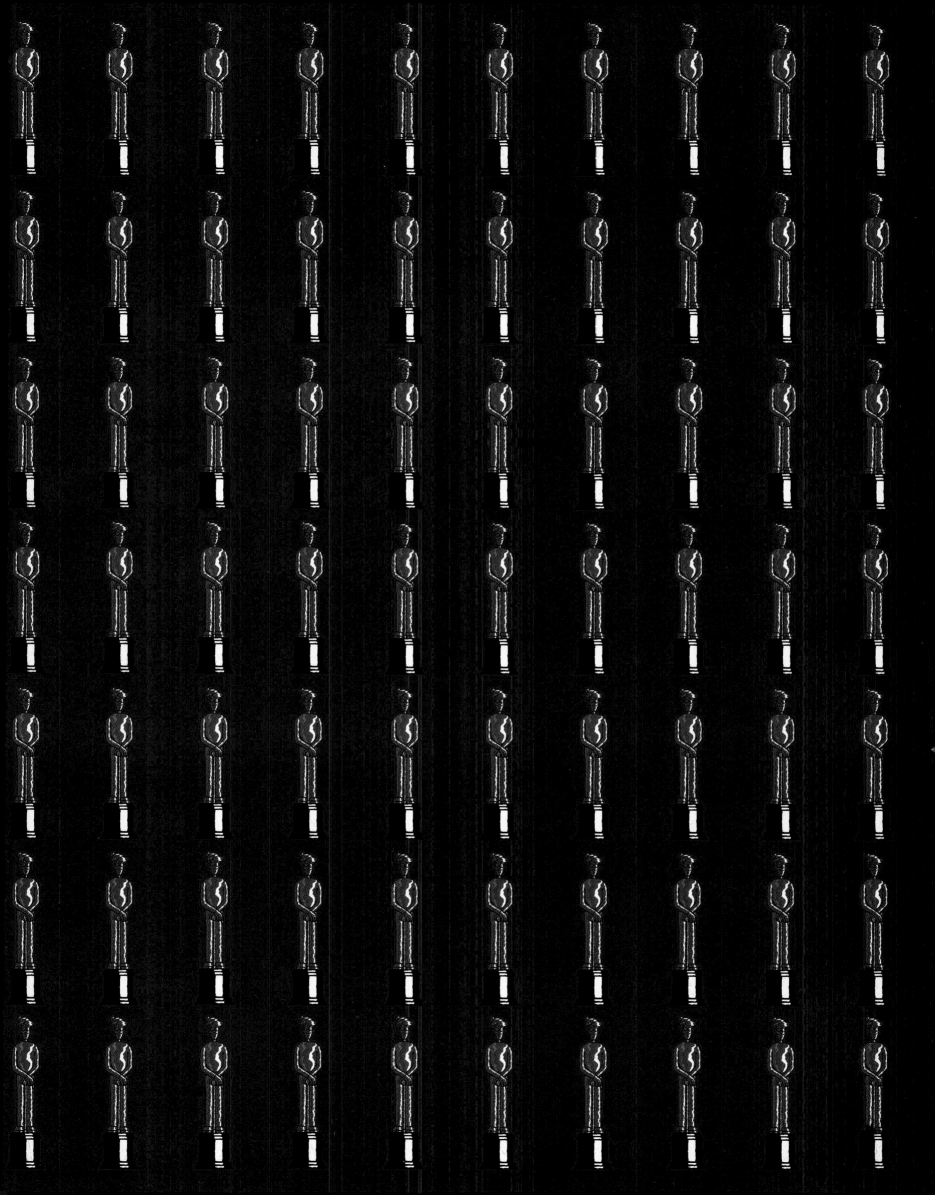

TO ELIZABETH, MIKE,
STEVE, EDDY AND TERRY
FOR ALL THEIR HELP
AND ENCOURAGEMENT

First published 1993 by Walker Books Ltd
87 Vauxhall Walk, London SE11 5HJ
This edition published 2016
22 24 26 28 30 29 27 25 23
© 1987 – 2016 Martin Handford

The right of Martin Handford to be identified as author/illustrator of this work has been
asserted by him in accordance with the Copyright, Designs and Patents Act 1988.
Use of the Hollywood sign™/© 1993 Hollywood Chamber of Commerce under license
authorized by Curtis Management Group, Indianapolis, Indiana, USA
King Kong © 1993 RKO Pictures, Inc. All rights reserved. Courtesy of Turner Entertainment Co.
This book has been typeset in Wallyfont and Optima.
Printed in China
All rights reserved.
British Library Cataloguing in Publication Data:
a catalogue record for this book is available from the British Library.
ISBN 978-1-4063-0588-3
www.walker.co.uk

WHERE'S WALLY? IN HOLLYWOOD

MARTIN HANDFORD

WALKER BOOKS
AND SUBSIDIARIES
LONDON · BOSTON · SYDNEY · AUCKLAND

A DREAM COME TRUE

WOW, WALLY-WATCHERS, THIS IS FANTASTIC, I'M REALLY IN HOLLYWOOD! LOOK AT THE FILM PEOPLE EVERYWHERE — I WONDER WHAT MOVIES THEY'RE MAKING. THIS IS MY DREAM COME TRUE ... TO MEET THE DIRECTORS AND ACTORS, TO WALK THROUGH THE CROWDS OF EXTRAS, TO SEE BEHIND THE SCENES! PHEW, I WONDER IF I'LL APPEAR IN A MOVIE MYSELF!

★ ★ ★ ★ WHAT TO LOOK FOR IN HOLLYWOOD! ★ ★ ★ ★

WELCOME TO TINSELTOWN, WALLY-WATCHERS! THESE ARE THE PEOPLE AND THINGS TO LOOK FOR AS YOU WALK THROUGH THE FILM SETS WITH WALLY.

★ FIRST (OF COURSE!) WHERE'S WALLY?

★ NEXT FIND WALLY'S CANINE COMPANION, WOOF — REMEMBER, ALL YOU CAN SEE IS HIS TAIL!

★ THEN FIND WALLY'S FRIEND, WENDA!

★ ABRACADABRA! NOW FOCUS IN ON WIZARD WHITEBEARD!

★ BOO! HISS! HERE COMES THE BAD GUY, ODLAW!

★ NOW SPOT THESE 25 WALLY-WATCHERS, EACH OF WHOM APPEARS ONLY ONCE BEFORE THE FINAL FANTASTIC SCENE!

★ WOW! INCREDIBLE! SPOT ONE OTHER CHARACTER WHO APPEARS IN EVERY SCENE EXCEPT THE LAST!

★ ★ KEEP ON SEARCHING! THERE'S MORE TO FIND! ★ ★

ON EVERY SET, FIND WALLY'S LOST KEY!

WOOF'S LOST BONE! WENDA'S LOST CAMERA! WIZARD WHITEBEARD'S SCROLL!

ODLAW'S LOST BINOCULARS! AND A MISSING CAN OF FILM!

★ ★ ★ ★ ★ ★ ★ AND MORE AND MORE! ★ ★ ★ ★ ★ ★ ★

EACH OF THE FOUR POSTERS ON THE WALL OVER THERE IS PART OF ONE OF THE FILM SETS WALLY IS ABOUT TO VISIT. ★ FIND OUT WHERE THE POSTERS CAME FROM. ★ THEN SPOT ANY DIFFERENCES BETWEEN THE POSTERS AND THE SETS.

SHHH! THIS IS A SILENT MOVIE

SO THIS IS HOW THE HOLLYWOOD DREAM BEGAN — WITH SILENT MOVIES MADE IN BLACK AND WHITE. IT LOOKS CRAZY AND IT MAKES YOU LAUGH. ACTING IN SLAPSTICK COMEDIES MUST BE REALLY HARD — LOOK HOW MANY ACCIDENTS ARE HAPPENING. BUT THE GREAT THING IS THAT NONE OF THE ACTORS EVER GET HURT, HOWEVER OFTEN THEY FALL FLAT ON THEIR FACES!

$10,000

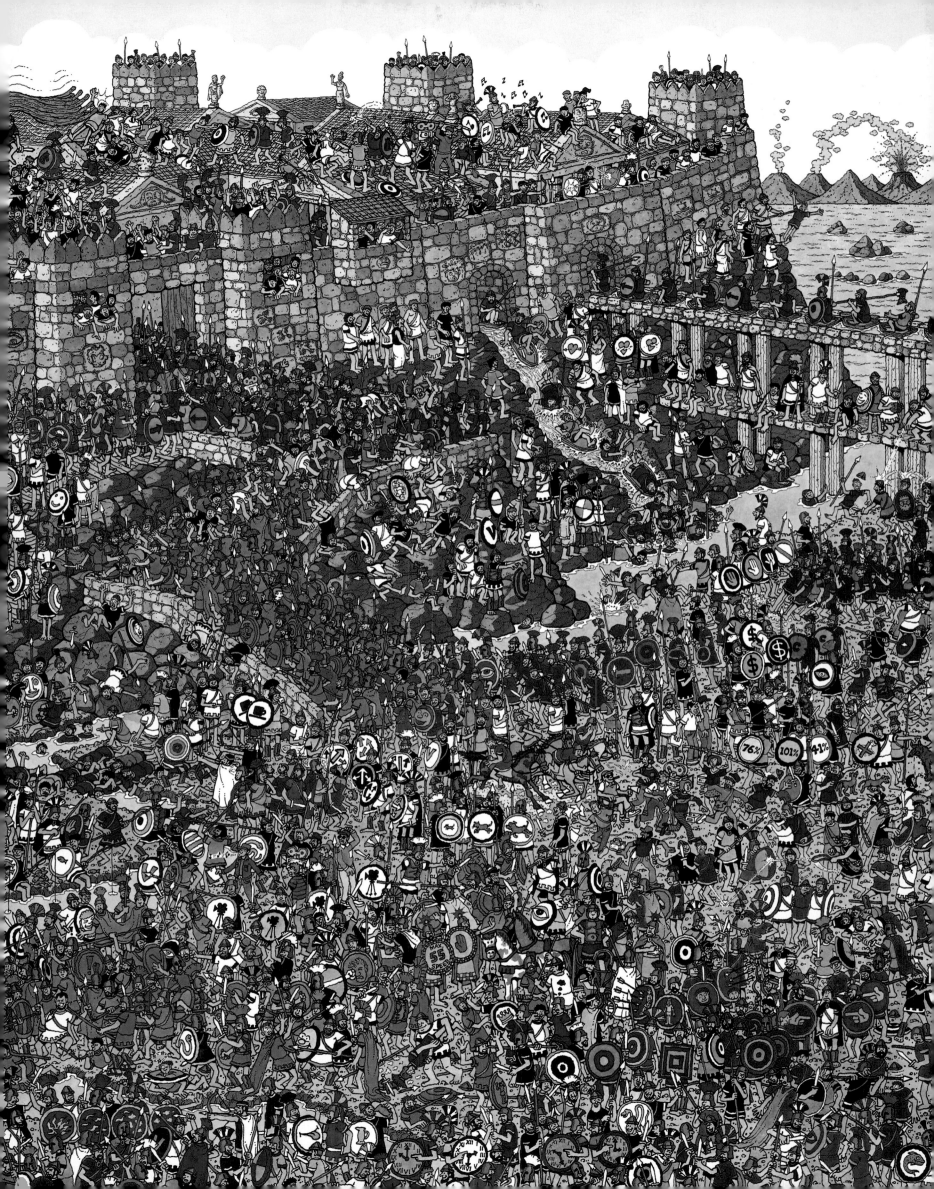

FUN IN THE FOREIGN LEGION

PHEW, FILM FANS, DON'T GET OVERHEATED, THIS IS
THE MOST SIZZLING LOCATION SO FAR! EVERYONE'S
SWELTERING, FROM STARS TO SAND-SHIFTERS. SOME
OF THOSE EXTRAS LOOK LIKE THEY'RE LOSING THEIR
COOL – HAVE THEY FORGOTTEN THIS IS ONLY A FILM?
PERHAPS IT'S TIME A FEW MORE OF THEM DESERTED
THE DESERT AND JOINED THE RUSH FOR ICE CREAM!

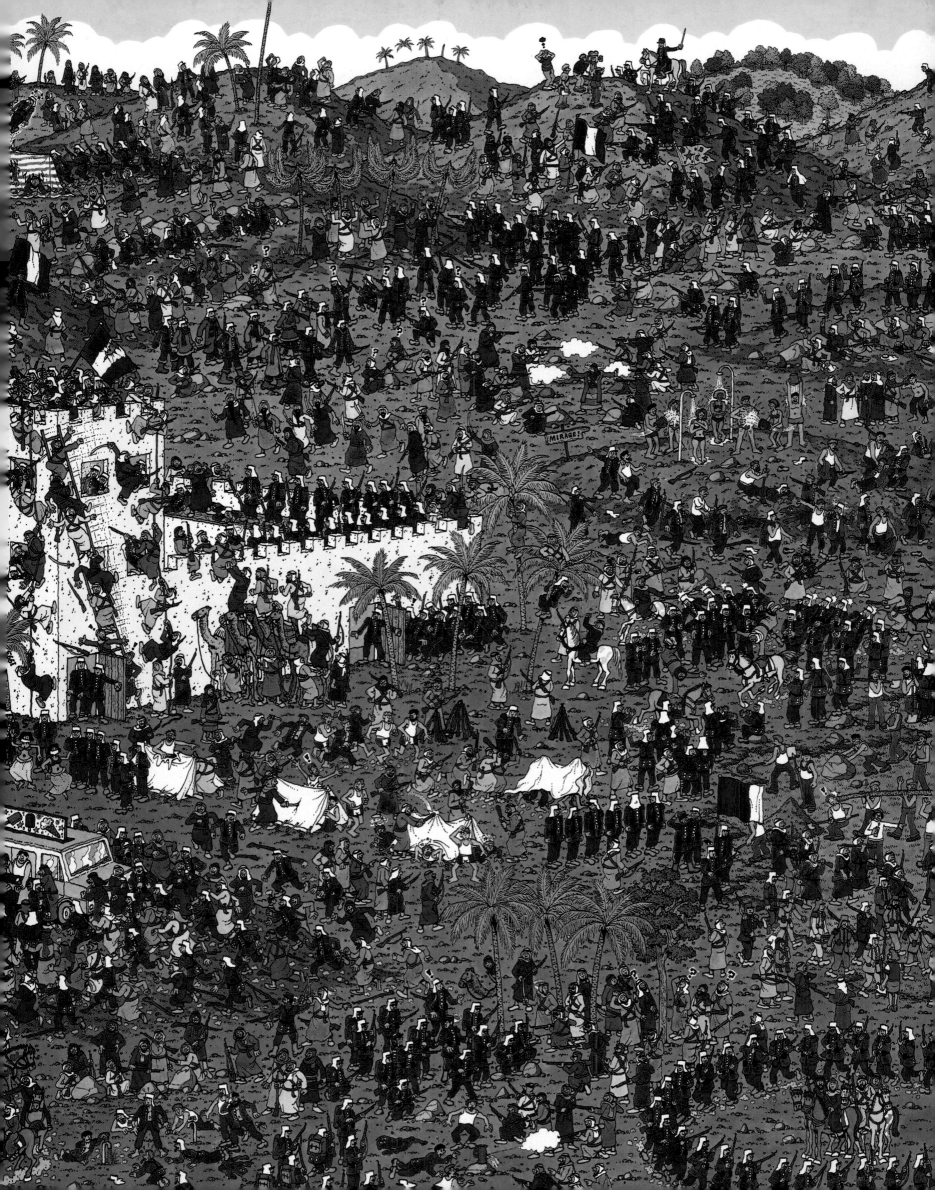

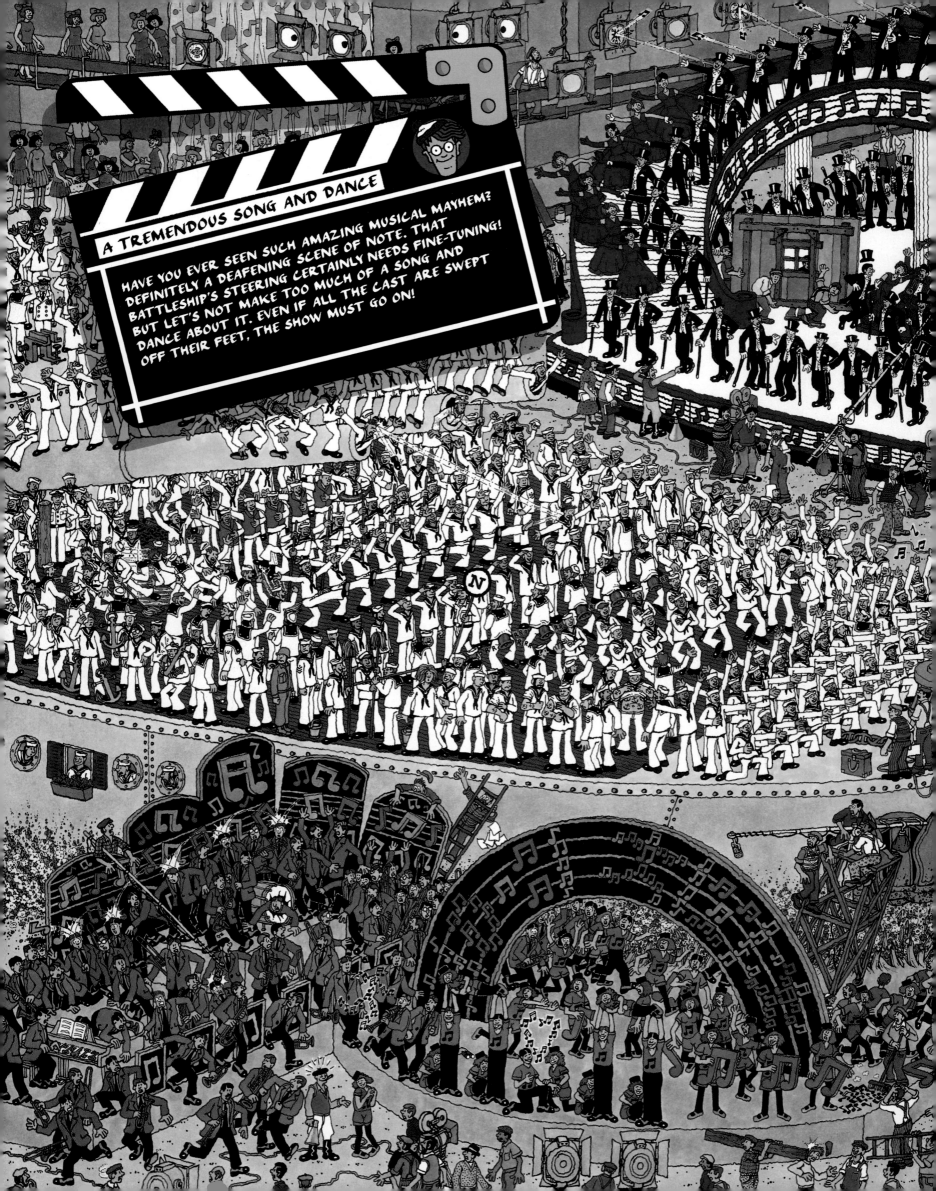

CAVE OF THE PLUNDERING PIRATES

WHAT A PLETHORA OF PLUNDERING PIRATES, WALLY-WATCHERS! WHAT A CRUSH IN THE CAVE! THERE MUST BE TONS OF TREATS AND TRINKETS IN THIS TEEMING TREASURE TROVE. WITH SPOOKY SPIRITS CENTRE STAGE AND PIRATICAL PILFERERS TO SPOT, THE DIRECTOR CERTAINLY HAS HIS HANDS FULL. LET'S HOPE HE HAS THE GOLDEN TOUCH! SHIVER-ME-TIMBERS, WHAT A FEARFULLY FUNNY FLICK THIS IS!

THE SWASHBUCKLING MUSKETEERS

ALL FOR ONE, ONE FOR ALL! – WASN'T THAT THE MOTTO OF THE THREE MUSKETEERS? NOW LOOK AT THIS FREE-FOR-ALL! CAN YOU SPOT OUR THREE GALLANT HEROES BATTLING WITH THE RED-COATED CARDINAL'S GUARDS? WITH ALL THIS SWASHBUCKLING ACTION GOING ON, I WONDER HOW THE CAMERAMEN CAN CAPTURE IT ALL ON FILM!

DINOSAURS, SPACEMEN AND GHOULS

PHEW, INCREDIBLE! TIME, SPACE AND HORROR ARE IN A MIGHTY MUDDLE HERE! WHAT COSMIC COSTUMES AND WHAT GREAT SPECIAL EFFECTS! ONE OF THOSE FLYING SAUCERS LOOKS LIKE IT'S REALLY FLYING! ARE THOSE REAL ALIENS INSIDE, NOT ACTORS AT ALL? SO WHAT'S REAL AND WHAT'S MADE UP IN FILMS LIKE THESE?

WHEN THE STARS COME OUT

WOW, WALLY-WATCHERS, THIS IS WHAT I CALL GLAMOUR! I'M AT A MAJOR MOVIE PREMIERE. THE STARS HAVE COME TO SEE THE FILM, THE CROWDS HAVE COME TO SEE THE STARS. LOOK AT THAT PINK STRETCH LIMO – NOW THAT'S A PROPER CAR FOR A STAR. AND WHO'S IN THE BONE-MOBILE BEHIND? AND DOESN'T KING KONG LOOK NICER IN LIFE THAN WHEN HE'S ON THE SCREEN?

WHERE'S WALLY? THE MUSICAL

WOW, WHAT AN EXTRAVAGANZA, WALLY-WATCHERS — THIS ALL-SINGING, ALL-DANCING MOVIE IS ALL ABOUT ME AND MY FRIENDS! LOOK HOW MANY ACTORS ARE DRESSED UP AS ME! AND LOOK AT ALL THE WOOFS, WENDAS, WIZARD WHITEBEARDS AND ODLAWS. HAVE YOU NOTICED THAT THE WARDROBE DEPARTMENT HAS MADE MISTAKES WITH SOME OF THE ACTORS' COSTUMES? BUT THAT WON'T HELP YOU FIND THE REAL ME AND MY FOUR FRIENDS IN THIS FILM! I'LL GIVE YOU SOME CLUES. I'M THE WALLY WITH SOMETHING EXTRA FOR WOOF. ALL YOU CAN SEE OF THE REAL WOOF IS HIS TAIL. THE REAL WENDA HAS A CAMERA. THE REAL WIZARD WHITEBEARD IS WEARING A HAT BENT TO THE LEFT. AND THE REAL ODLAW IS HOLDING A WALKING STICK.
THERE'S JUST ONE MORE THING. I'VE BEEN FOLLOWED HERE BY ONE CHARACTER FROM EVERY SET I'VE VISITED. SO CAN YOU SPOT ALL ELEVEN OF THEM IN THIS SCENE? AND CAN YOU FIND OUT WHEN EACH CHARACTER FIRST JOINED ME; AND CATCH ALL THEIR APPEARANCES THROUGHOUT MY TRAVELS?

GREETINGS,
WALLY FOLLOWERS!
WOW, THE BEACH WAS
GREAT TODAY! ALL
AROUND ME I SAW
STRIPES ON TOWELS,
CLOTHES, UMBRELLAS,
AND BEACH HUTS.
THERE WAS A SAND-
CASTLE WITH A REAL
KNIGHT IN ARMOUR
INSIDE! FANTASTIC!

Wally

TO:
WALLY FOLLOWERS,
HERE, THERE,
EVERYWHERE.

WAKEY, WAKEY, WALLY FRIENDS!
HAVE YOU EVER SEEN MERMAIDS
IN A CANAL? OR FLOWERS
PAINTED ALL OVER A TENT?
OR A LINE OF HIKERS WINDING
ALONG THE COUNTRY LANES?
I HAVE. TODAY. IT WAS
JUST AMAZING!

Wally

TO:
WALLY'S FRIENDS,
NORTH OF THE SOUTH POLE,
EAST OF THE WEST POLE,
THE WORLD.

WHERE'S CAMP SITE WALLY?

WELCOME, WALLY-WATCHERS!
I SAW SOME UNFORGETTABLE
SIGHTS TODAY: LOTS OF
RAILS AND TABLES FULL OF
COLOURFUL THINGS; SOME
DEMONSTRATIONS GOING
WRONG; A MAN CHECKING A
WASHING MACHINE BY WASHING
HIS OWN CLOTHES IN IT FIRST.
PHEW! INCREDIBLE!

Wally

WHERE'S
DEPARTMENT
STORE
WALLY?

TO:
WALLY-WATCHERS,
OVER THE MOON,
THE WILD WEST,
NOW.

ROLL UP, WALLY FUN LOVERS!
WOW! I'VE LOST ALL MY
THINGS, ONE IN EVERY PLACE
I'VE VISITED. NOW YOU HAVE
TO GO BACK AND FIND THEM.
AND SOMEWHERE ONE OF
THE WALLY-WATCHERS HAS
LOST THE BOBBLE FROM HIS
HAT. CAN YOU SPOT WHICH
ONE, AND FIND THE MISSING
BOBBLE?

Wally

TO:
WALLY FUN LOVERS,
BACK TO THE
BEGINNING,
START AGAIN,
TERRIFIC.

THE GREAT WHERE'S WALLY? CHECKLIST
Hundreds more things for Wally-watchers to watch out for!

IN TOWN
- A dog on a roof
- A man on a fountain
- A man about to trip over a dog's lead
- A car crash
- A keen barber
- People in a street, watching television
- A puncture caused by an arrow
- A tearful tune
- A boy attacked by a plant
- A sandwich
- A waiter who isn't concentrating
- Two firemen waving at each other
- A face on a wall
- A man coming out of a man hole
- A man feeding birds

SKI SLOPES
- A man reading on a roof
- A flying skier
- A runaway skier
- A backward skier
- A portrait in snow
- An illegal fisherman
- Five people wearing stripy scarves
- Snow about to fall on two laughing men
- Three skiers who have hit trees
- An Alpine horn
- Two broken flagpoles
- A flag collector
- Four people in yellow-hooded tops
- A skier up a tree
- A water skier on snow
- A Yeti
- Two skiing reindeer
- A roof jumper
- Someone crashing through five skiers

THE RAILWAY STATION
- Four shovels and five spades
- A trolley carrying five suitcases
- People being knocked over by a door
- A man about to step on a ball
- Three different times at the same time
- A wheelbarrow pram
- A face on a train
- Five people reading one newspaper
- A show-off with a suitcase
- Someone tripping over a dog
- Two men with red-and-white-striped ties
- A smoking train
- A squeeze on a bench
- A dog tearing a man's trousers
- A man sitting on a suitcase
- Twenty cows
- Someone struggling to lift a suitcase
- Two suitcases spilling their contents
- A broken weighing machine

ON THE BEACH
- A dog and its owners wearing sunglasses
- A man who is overdressed
- A muscular medallion man
- A water skier
- A stripy photographer
- A punctured lilo
- A donkey who likes ice cream
- A man being squashed
- A punctured beach ball
- A human pyramid
- Three people reading newspapers
- A cowboy
- A human donkey
- A radio
- A cross-looking human stepping-stone
- A red lilo
- Age and beauty
- Two red-and-yellow umbrellas
- Two men with vests, one without
- A show-off with sandcastles
- Someone wearing braces
- A cream coloured dog
- Three protruding tongues
- Two oddly fitting hats
- Five sprinters
- A towel with a hole in it
- A punctured hovercraft
- A boy who's not allowed any ice cream
- Two caps with extra-long peaks

CAMP SITE
- A bull in a hedge
- Bull horns
- A shark in a canal
- A bull seeing red
- A careless kick
- Tea in a lap
- A low bridge
- A person knocked over by a mallet
- A man surprised undressing
- A bicycle tyre about to be punctured
- Six dogs
- A scarecrow that doesn't work
- A wigwam
- Large biceps
- Three campers with very long beards
- A collapsed tent
- A smoking barbecue
- A fisherman catching old boots
- A winning penny-farthing
- A boy scout making fire
- A roller hiker
- A man blowing up a dinghy
- Thirsty walkers
- Runners on the road
- A bull chasing two people
- A camper's butler

AIRPORT
- A flying saucer
- A boy sitting with the revolving luggage
- A leaking fuel pipe
- Flight controllers playing badminton
- A rocket
- A tower on top of the control tower
- Three watch smugglers
- An airport worker resting on a plane
- A forklift truck
- A wind-sock
- Someone with a bucket and spade
- Six air hostesses in light blue uniforms
- A plane with giant tail wings
- A fire engine and ten firemen
- Two passengers wearing white hats
- A plane that doesn't fly
- A flying Ace
- A pen and paper
- Runners on a runway
- Five men blowing up a balloon
- Dracula
- Three childish pilots
- Eighteen airport workers with yellow caps

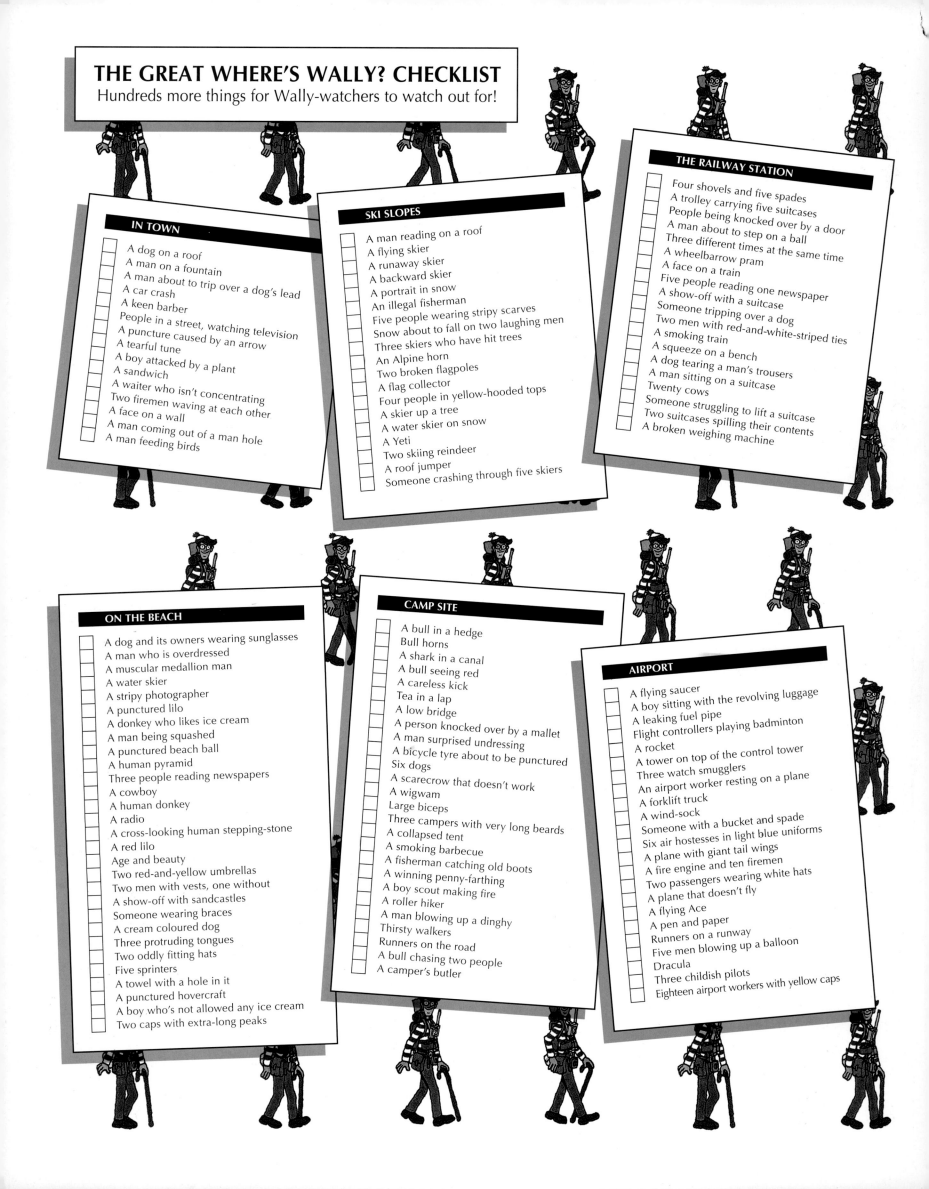

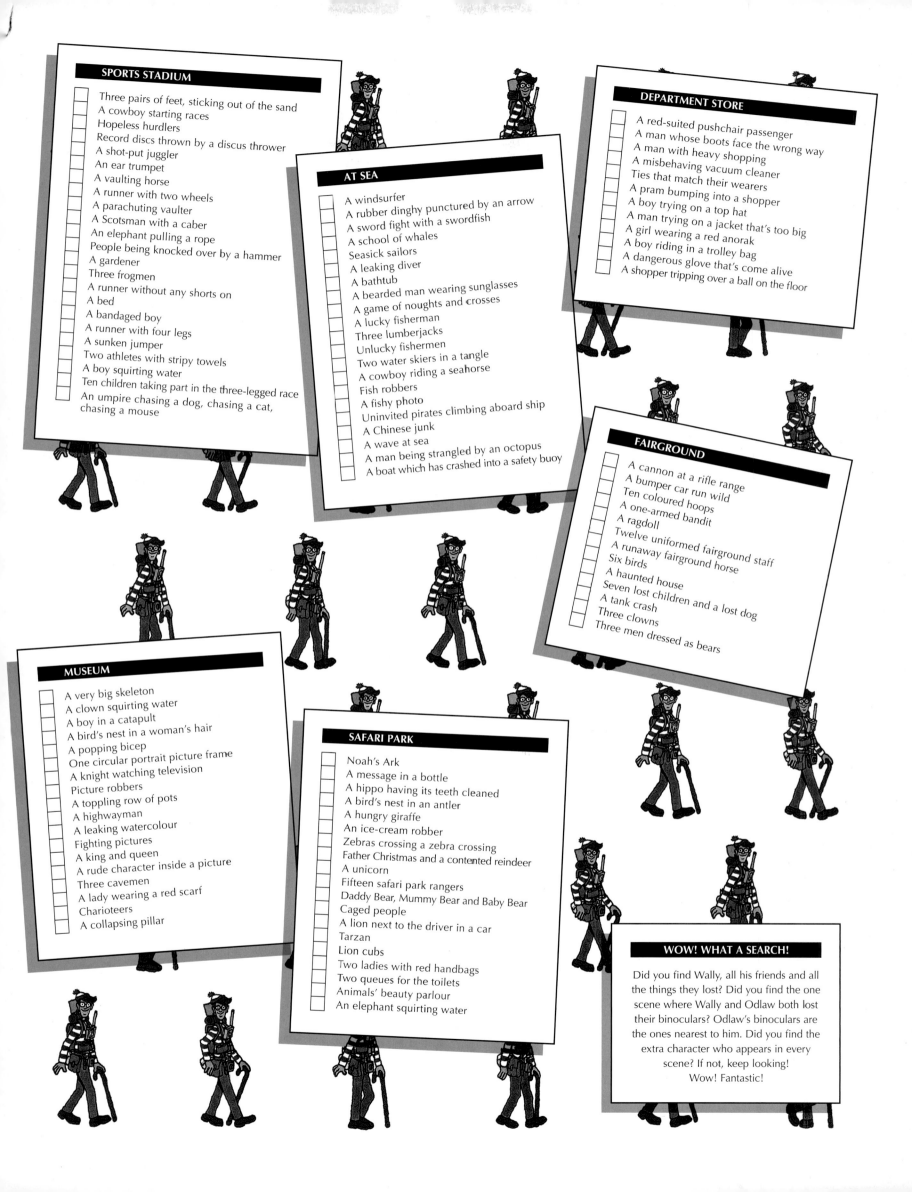

SPORTS STADIUM

- Three pairs of feet, sticking out of the sand
- A cowboy starting races
- Hopeless hurdlers
- Record discs thrown by a discus thrower
- A shot-put juggler
- An ear trumpet
- A vaulting horse
- A runner with two wheels
- A parachuting vaulter
- A Scotsman with a caber
- An elephant pulling a rope
- People being knocked over by a hammer
- A gardener
- Three frogmen
- A runner without any shorts on
- A bed
- A bandaged boy
- A runner with four legs
- A sunken jumper
- Two athletes with stripy towels
- A boy squirting water
- Ten children taking part in the three-legged race
- An umpire chasing a dog, chasing a cat, chasing a mouse

AT SEA

- A windsurfer
- A rubber dinghy punctured by an arrow
- A sword fight with a swordfish
- A school of whales
- Seasick sailors
- A leaking diver
- A bathtub
- A bearded man wearing sunglasses
- A game of noughts and crosses
- A lucky fisherman
- Three lumberjacks
- Unlucky fishermen
- Two water skiers in a tangle
- A cowboy riding a seahorse
- Fish robbers
- A fishy photo
- Uninvited pirates climbing aboard ship
- A Chinese junk
- A wave at sea
- A man being strangled by an octopus
- A boat which has crashed into a safety buoy

DEPARTMENT STORE

- A red-suited pushchair passenger
- A man whose boots face the wrong way
- A man with heavy shopping
- A misbehaving vacuum cleaner
- Ties that match their wearers
- A pram bumping into a shopper
- A boy trying on a top hat
- A man trying on a jacket that's too big
- A girl wearing a red anorak
- A boy riding in a trolley bag
- A dangerous glove that's come alive
- A shopper tripping over a ball on the floor

FAIRGROUND

- A cannon at a rifle range
- A bumper car run wild
- Ten coloured hoops
- A one-armed bandit
- A ragdoll
- Twelve uniformed fairground staff
- A runaway fairground horse
- Six birds
- A haunted house
- Seven lost children and a lost dog
- A tank crash
- Three clowns
- Three men dressed as bears

MUSEUM

- A very big skeleton
- A clown squirting water
- A boy in a catapult
- A bird's nest in a woman's hair
- A popping bicep
- One circular portrait picture frame
- A knight watching television
- Picture robbers
- A toppling row of pots
- A highwayman
- A leaking watercolour
- Fighting pictures
- A king and queen
- A rude character inside a picture
- Three cavemen
- A lady wearing a red scarf
- Charioteers
- A collapsing pillar

SAFARI PARK

- Noah's Ark
- A message in a bottle
- A hippo having its teeth cleaned
- A bird's nest in an antler
- A hungry giraffe
- An ice-cream robber
- Zebras crossing a zebra crossing
- Father Christmas and a contented reindeer
- A unicorn
- Fifteen safari park rangers
- Daddy Bear, Mummy Bear and Baby Bear
- Caged people
- A lion next to the driver in a car
- Tarzan
- Lion cubs
- Two ladies with red handbags
- Two queues for the toilets
- Animals' beauty parlour
- An elephant squirting water

WOW! WHAT A SEARCH!

Did you find Wally, all his friends and all the things they lost? Did you find the one scene where Wally and Odlaw both lost their binoculars? Odlaw's binoculars are the ones nearest to him. Did you find the extra character who appears in every scene? If not, keep looking!
Wow! Fantastic!